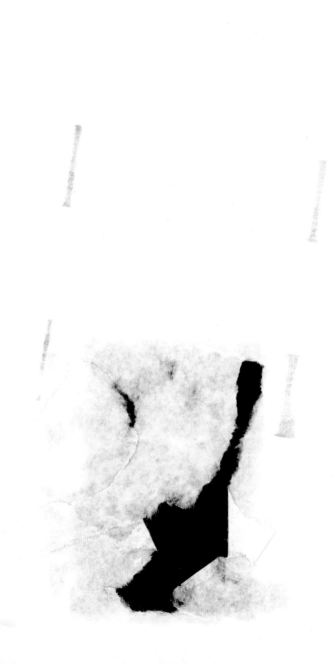

CLASSICS OF RUSSIAN POETRY

Alexander Pushkin

LITTLE TRAGEDIES

"Translators are the post-horses of civilization"
A. S. Pushkin, 1830

ALEXANDER PUSHKIN
Little Tragedies

translated from the Russian
by Eugene M. Kayden

illustrated by
Vladimir Favorsky

The Antioch Press
Yellow Springs, Ohio • 1965

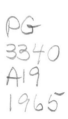
First edition
January 1965

Copyright 1965 by Eugene M. Kayden. Library of Congress Catalog Card No. 62-21071. Printed in the United States of America.

DEDICATED

TO

MY BROTHER

SIMON

TO DEAR MEMORIES OF BOYHOOD YEARS

Contents

THE
COVETOUS
KNIGHT

SCENE I

ALBERT AND JEAN
IN A TOWER

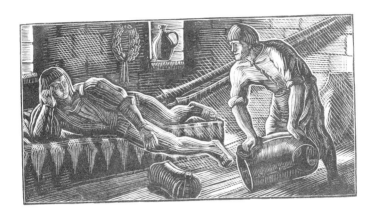

ALBERT

No matter what the cost, I will not miss
The tournament. Show me my helmet, Jean.
(Jean brings him the helmet.)
It is a wreck, pierced through and through. I have
No use for it. I'll need another helmet.
O what a stroke! That cursèd Count de Lorge!

JEAN

But you, I'll say, did soundly pay him back.
For after you had bounced him off his horse,
He lay like dead a day and night. I doubt
He is recovered.

ALBERT

     Yet, he has no loss,
For his Venetian breastplate is as good
As new. His fall means nothing in the end,
No burden of unusual expense.
I should have seized his helmet on the spot,
I should have made it mine, but was ashamed
Before the ladies and the Duke. A plague
Upon the Count! I wish that he had pierced
My skull; I prized my only helmet more.
Besides, I need some clothes. Last time our knights
Were seated all in satin and in velvet
At the Duke's table, but I alone appeared
In my coat-of-mail. I excused myself;
I'd come upon the tournament by chance,
I made it plain. But what shall I say now?
Poverty! How it shames me in the world!
When Count de Lorge by rushing forward pierced
My helmet with his heavy lance, then I,
Bareheaded, like the wind flew after him
And hurled him down some twenty paces back
As though he were a little page. How all
The ladies rose, amazed, when fair Clotilda
Herself cried out against her will in fear,
And all the heralds praised aloud my stroke!
But not a soul among them understood
The cause of all that bravery and might!
My ruined helmet, not my daring, roused
My fury; greed at home, not courage, greed!
That sordid love of gain at home—beneath

My father's roof—corruption manifest!
But how's poor Emir doing?

JEAN

                       Lame, still lame;
It would not do to ride him for a while.

ALBERT

There's little I can do but buy the bay
Meanwhile, and luckily the price is low.

JEAN

And still we do not have the price to pay.

ALBERT

That scoundrel Solomon, what does he say?

JEAN

He says he can't keep lending you unless
You offer good security.

ALBERT

                  The devil!
And where am I to find security?

JEAN

That's what I told him.

ALBERT

              And—

JEAN

                 He groans and mumbles.

ALBERT

You should have told him then my father's rich

As any Jew, and at his death I'll be
In time his only heir.

JEAN

So I told him.

ALBERT
And then?

JEAN

He mumbles and he groans.

ALBERT

What luck!

JEAN
He said he'd come himself.

ALBERT

Thank God for that.
I'll never let him free without a ransom.
(*A knock on the door.*)
Who's there?

(*Jew enters.*)

JEW

Your humble servant.

ALBERT

Ah, a friend!
The cursèd Jew, our worthy Solomon!
Come in. I understand you will not grant
Another loan on trust.

JEW

My gracious knight!
Upon my word I'd gladly lend, but cannot.
Where find the money? I am a ruined man
Since I have helped your knights so long with loans.
But who pays back on time? I've come to ask
If you might not repay a part. . . .

ALBERT

Robber!
If I had cash about me, do you think
I'd bother here with you? Be fair, I say!
And why be obstinate, friend Solomon?
Out with your ducats! Lend a hundred now
Or I will have you searched.

JEW

A hundred ducats!
Where shall I find a hundred, eh?

ALBERT

Listen!
Have you no shame, denying to a friend
Your help in time?

JEW

I swear to you!

ALBERT

Come, come,
What surety do you want? Man, what nonsense!
What bond, what surety? Would a pig skin do?
Had I anything at all to give or pledge,
I would have sold it long ago. You dog,
Is not a knight's true word enough?

7

JEW

                              Your word
As long as you're alive means much, yes, much.
The treasure chests of Flanders' richest men
Your word will open like a talisman.
But if to one poor Jew like me you give
Your word alone in pledge, and meantime die
(Which God forbid), it would be like a key
To a rich casket sunk beneath the sea.

ALBERT

You mean to say my father might outlive me?

JEW

Who knows the count of days we do not own?
A youth but yesternight, and dead today,
And four old men on stooping shoulders bear
His body to the grave. The baron lives.
And God may grant him, mind you, many years—
Ten, twenty, twenty-five, or maybe thirty.

ALBERT

You lie, you Jew! In thirty years from now
I shall be fifty—and too old. What use
Would money be to me?

JEW

                         You say what use?
Money?—But money's good at any age!
In youth we think it is a ready servant
And carelessly we spend it here and there.
When old, you have it as your faithful friend,
To guard it like the apple of your eye.

ALBERT

No servant, no! nor friend, my father's money!
Alas, his gold's the overlord he serves
And serves in faith, like an Algerian slave,
Like a chained hound. In his unheated kennel
He lives alone, on water, crusts of bread,—
For nights awake to run about and snarl.
Meanwhile his gold lies buried—idle gold
In secret chests. But mark! It shall be mine
Someday, and then my servant shall not sleep.

JEW

Ah, yes, upon the day his lordship dies,
Those coins will flow more plentiful than tears.
May fortune make you soon his heir.

ALBERT

                                            Amen!

JEW

It may be—

ALBERT

         What?

JEW

                       There is another chance,
Another way perhaps.

ALBERT

                       What way, what chance?

JEW

I know a little Jew, a queer old man,
A poor apothecary. . . .

ALBERT

                              Oh, like you,
A usurer! Or is he honest, what?

JEW

My lord, Tobiah drives a different trade.
He blends some drops . . . really, a magic thing
In its effects.

ALBERT

                     What use his drops for me?

JEW

A glass of water, then three drops, no more;
They have no taste, nor color. He who drinks
Them off, without a fit or stomach pain,
Without a trace of suffering will die.

ALBERT

Your queer old man sells poison?

JEAN

                              Also poison.

ALBERT

I see. You offer then instead of gold
A loan of poison, some two hundred vials,
A vial for each ducat. Am I right?

JEW

It pleases you too well to laugh at me.
But no! . . . perhaps I'm wrong . . . I thought that you
Perhaps believed the Baron's near his death.

ALBERT

    What! Poison, kill my father! And you dare
    To me, his son, to my face! ... Hold him, Jean!
    And do you know, you devil of a Jew,
    You cur, you snake, I'll have you hanged at once
    Upon our gate for this!

JEW

                         My lord, I grieve
    For jesting thus. Forgive me.

ALBERT

                            Jean, a rope.

JEW

I . . . I was jesting. I have the money here.

ALBERT

Out, out, you dog!

(The Jew leaves.)

O wretched me! 'Tis all
My father's greed! The Jew has dared to hint
His death to me! Give me a glass of wine!
I'm in a fever. . . . Jean, I still must have
That money. Run, and stop the cursed Jew!
Accept his ducats. Bring my inkhorn, Jean.
I'll give the villain his receipt. . . . Don't let
That Judas in again. . . . No, wait! I fear,
His coins will always reek to me of poison,
As did the coins the other Judas took. . . .
I asked for wine!

JEAN

There's not a drop.

ALBERT

I mean
What Raymond sent from Spain—his gift to me.

JEAN

Last night I took the one remaining bottle
To our sick blacksmith.

ALBERT

Yes, I now remember.
Then fetch me water. What a wretched life!
My mind's made up. I'll ask the Duke himself

For justice. Let him make my father treat
Me as a rightful son, not as a rat
Begotten in a cellar.

SCENE II

Vaulted Cellar

The Baron

As a young scamp who waits the trysting hour
With some intriguing harlot or little fool
He has seduced, thus I await daylong
And dream of going down at last into
This vaulted darkness to my secret chests.
O happy hour! This evening I will leave
In coffer six, the one half empty still,
One handful of accumulated gold.
A trifle, true, but by such little sums
My treasures grow. There is a story told
About a king who ordered all his troops
To gather earth by handfuls in a heap
Day after day, and soon a hill rose high
Whereon the king could contemplate with joy
The plain white-dotted with his soldiers' tents
And watch the ships that ran upon the sea.
Thus, bit by bit, by handfuls I've been bringing
My customary tribute to this vault.
I've raised my hill at last, and from its height
At leisure I survey my wealth and power.
And who can set their limits? Like some demon,
From here in secret I can rule the world.

I've but to wish,—a palace will arise,
And in my splendid gardens there will throng
Fair companies of nymphs in airy dances;
The sacred muses, too, will pay their tribute;
Free genius will be my willing bondsman;
And noble virtue and unsleeping labor
Will humbly look to me for their reward.
I've but to whistle,—at my knees will cringe
Submissive, timid, blood-bespattered Crime,
And lick my hand, and, watchful, gaze into
My eyes to read my wishes by their glance.
All things obey me; I alone am free.
I am beyond desire, beyond all care,
All fear. I know my power, and in my knowledge
I am sufficient. . . .

(He looks into his money-bag.)

It seems a little sum,
But who can scan the tale of human woes,
Deception, curses, prayers, bitter tears
They represent like solemn deputies? . . .
I've here an old doubloon. This very day
A widow paid a debt, but first of all
She had to kneel beneath my window, wailing,
With her three children through the morning hours.
The rain came down, and ceased, and came again.
The shamming creature never budged; I might
Have driven her away, but yet I felt
She'd brought the money that her husband owed,
Afraid, no doubt, she'd be in jail next day.
And then this coin, Thibault's old debt! The fox,

Where did he get it from, that lazy rascal?
Stole it, I'm sure of that; perhaps—somewhere,
At nightfall, on the highway, in the woods. . . .
Ah, yes! If all the tears, the sweat, and blood
Shed in the world by men because of gold
I'm hoarding here, should from the earth gush forth,
We'd have a second flood, and I should perish
In my own secret cellar. Well, 'tis time.

(*He starts to unlock the chest.*)

Each night I come here to unlock my chest,
I feel all hot with trembling and with fear.
Not fear, no, no! (Whom should I fear? I keep
My trusty sword beside me, and its blade
Will guard my treasures.) Still a strange sensation
Hovers mysteriously and grips my heart. . . .
Physicians tell us, there are men who find
In acts of violence a sense of pleasure.
When I insert the key into the lock,
I likewise feel what murderers must feel
Who plunge the knife into a victim—pleasure
And terror all at once.

(*He opens the chest.*)

My blessed kingdom!

(*He pours in the coins.*)

At home at last! You've roamed enough about
The world in service to the lusts of men.
Here you shall sleep the sleep of peace and power
At last, like gods in quiet azure deeps. . . .
Tonight I wish to hold a mighty feast:

A candle shining brightly at each chest,
Each coffer open wide, and I myself
With eyes aglow upon my hill of splendor!

> (*He lights candles before the open chests.*)

Now I am king!—What magic light! How great
My realm, my subjects faithful to my will!
Here is my bliss, my honor; here, my fame!
Now I am a king! . . . But who will after me
Enjoy this bounty when I die? My heir!
That youthful madcap, spendthrift boy, of rakes
And revellers about the boon companion!
At my last hour, him, him these walls will hear
Beneath the peace and silence of the vault,—
Him and his crew of greedy, fawning courtiers.

He'll rob my body, steal the keys, and here
With peals of laughter open every coffer,
And all the treasures of my life will flow
Through satin pockets gaping to the winds.
Thus will a waster smash the sacred vessels,
And spill an oil that should anoint a king.
He'll play the merry spendthrift—by what right? . . .
Did I for nothing, as a gift, my wealth
Acquire? or in the way of gambling sport
By rattling dice and raking in the spoil?
Who knows how much of bitter self-denial,
What rebel passions tamed, what pain, what gloom,
What days of care and sleepless nights, my wealth
Has cost me? Yet my son will say, no doubt,
My heart with hoary moss was overgrown,
That I have had no longings, never felt
The silent voice of conscience in my life,—
Yes, conscience, that sharp-toothed beast that scrapes
About the heart, that fierce intruding guest,
That wearisome companion, that creditor
Most brutish, worst of witches at whose call
The moon grows dark, the tombs move restlessly
And vomit forth their dead upon the night!
No, win by suffering your way to wealth
And then we'll see how any wretch would dare
To waste at will the treasures won by blood!
Oh, that I might conceal this vaulted chamber
From shameful eyes and from my grave arise,
And like a watchful shade come here to brood
Above my chests, and from all men defend
My treasures, even as I protect them now! . . .

SCENE III

IN THE DUKE'S CASTLE

ALBERT

Believe me, Sire, I've suffered long the shame
Of bitter poverty; in my despair
And helplessness I bring this charge of mine.

DUKE

I do believe, I do. A noble knight,
A man like you, would not accuse his father
Except in real distress; such knaves are few.
Then be at peace. I shall myself exhort
Your father gently. It's been many years
Since last we met. But I remember well
How he would seat me as a boy astride
His horse and cover playfully my head
With his heavy helm as with a bell.

(*Looks out of the window.*)

Who comes?
Your father?

ALBERT

He, my lord.

DUKE

Then get at once
Into this room. I'll call you soon.

(*Albert goes out. Baron enters.*)

Baron,
I'm glad to see you looking hale and hearty.

BARON

    I'm happy, Sire, I can in my old age
    Again present myself at your command.

DUKE

    Baron, it's much too long since we have met.
    Do you remember me?

BARON

                    Remember, Sire?
    I see you clear as now, a lively youngster.
    The Duke, your father, used to say to me:
    'Philip'—he always called me Philip,—'well,
    What say you, eh? In twenty years or so
    Both you and I will be like dolts to that
    Young stripling' . . . meaning you.

DUKE

                  Then let's renew
    Our friendship now. You never are at court.

BARON

    I'm old and feeble, Sire. Why should I be
    At court? The festive days and tournaments
    Are for the young. Their fun's no joy at my
    Old age. . . . If there be war, I'm ready, groaning,
    To get upon my horse again. I'll find
    Enough of strength to draw my ancient sword
    With trembling hands to fight in your defence.

DUKE

    Baron, I know your loyal heart. You were
    My grandfather's old friend; my father, too,
    Has known you well, and I have always held

You as a faithful knight and brave. Be seated.
And have you children, Baron?

BARON

An only son.

DUKE

Why do I never see him at our court?
I think it's worthy, fitting at his age,
His class, his station to attend us here.

BARON

My son dislikes a life of noise and mirth.
He has a timid, gloomy mind and likes
To roam around the castle in the woods
Forever like a fawn.

DUKE

It is not right
To shun the world. We can accustom him
In little time to tournaments and balls
And courtly joy. Send him to me; bestow
Some proper maintenance upon your son. . . .
I see you frown. Perhaps your coming here
Has worn you out.

BARON

I am not weary, Sire!
Your words bewilder me. I should not make
Before you this confession; yet your words
Compel me now to let you know some facts
About my son I gladly would conceal.
I fear, I regret he is unworthy, Sire,
To have your gracious favor and regard.

He whiles away his youth in common brawls,
In basest vice.

DUKE

     The reason—do believe me,
Baron, his lonely life. Both solitude
And idleness strike at the roots of youth.
Send him to me. I feel he will outgrow
The reckless habits born of loneliness.

BARON

Forgive me, Sire, I must in truth declare
I cannot give my free consent to this.

DUKE

But why?

BARON

    I pray you, let an old man go.

DUKE

No, I insist; give me the reason for your
Denying now my wish.

BARON

      My anger, Sire,
Against my son.

DUKE

    For what?

BARON

      His wicked crimes.

DUKE

What crimes, what acts of violence, in short?

BARON

I pray you, spare me, Sire!

DUKE

'Tis very strange!
You feel ashamed of him?

BARON

Ah, yes, ashamed. . . .

DUKE

For what offence, what act?

BARON

He . . . he did wish
To kill me.

DUKE

Kill you! I'll deliver him
To justice even now, the fiendish wretch!

BARON

I will not try to prove it, Sire, although
I know he fully wants to see me dead.
I know that he has tried so many times
To—

DUKE

What?

BARON

To rob me.

(*Albert rushes into the room.*)

ALBERT

Baron, that's a lie!

DUKE

(*To the son*)

How dare you?

BARON

You, you here! You dare—to me!
To me, your father! such a word to me! . . .
I lie? To say to me, before our sovereign! . . .
Am I no more a knight?

ALBERT

A liar, yes!

BARON

O God of justice, where Thy thunderbolts?
Take this, and let the sword decide my cause.

(*He throws down his glove; his son picks it up.*)

ALBERT

I thank you. This, my father's first real gift.

DUKE

What do I see? I can't believe it true!
A son accepts the challenge of his father!
In what a cruel age have I assumed
The crown of dukes! Silence! You, madman, you!
And you, young tiger-cub! Have done at once!
Return the glove to me!

(*He takes it away from Albert.*)

ALBERT

(*aside*)

This is a pity.

DUKE

  You pounced upon it with your claws! Monster!
  Begone! and do not dare to show yourself
  Before me till I please to call you back.

  (*Albert leaves.*)

  And you, unhappy man, so old, have you
  No shame?

BARON

              I'm tired, tired! Do forgive me, Sire!
  I'm stifled . . . air . . . more air! Where are the keys?
  My keys, my keys! . . .

DUKE

              He's dead. O God in heaven!
  O what a dreadful age! What dreadful hearts!

MOZART
AND
SALIERI

SCENE I

Room in Salieri's House

Salieri
Men say there is no justice in the world.
I know there's none in heaven, and, to my mind,
The fact is clear as any simple scale.
I've loved the art of music from my birth;
As a boy, when the great resounding organ
Swelled wave on wave about me in the church,
I listened long, enraptured, and sweet tears,
Sweet and involuntary tears, I wept.
I spurned the games that boys are wont to play;
All learning, all save music, I despised
As futile matter, and turned away with pride
And obstinate disdain in my devotion
To music, music only. My way was hard
At first, but steadily I overcame

Each hardship in my search for craftsmanship
Through discipline,—the basis of true art.
My skill I've gained by work, my fingers trained
To strict precision, rigid faithfulness.
I then dissected music like a corpse,
Proved harmony by scientific rules;
Then only, learned in my craft, I dared
To crave the rapture of creative fancy.
I worked with zeal, secluded from the world,
And did not dare to dream of fame and glory.
Forgetting food and sleep, three days on end,
As one at worship in a cell, often
I knew the tears and joy of inspiration;
Yet, coldly critical, I'd burn my work
And watch it vanish in a wisp of smoke,—
Myself the maker and myself the judge.
Nay, even more: When the immortal Gluck
Appeared, revealing unto us profound
Enchanting harmonies, did I not forsake
All I had loved and served with burning faith?
I followed him, unmurmuring, as a man
Who'd walked with error in a lampless world,
Then found a master lighting the new way.
I reached, by stubborn work and resolution,
In the immeasurable realm of art
A lofty place. The world at last received
My work and harmonies with sympathy
And praise. My cup of happiness was full.
I have rejoiced in fortune, peace, and fame;
I have rejoiced in the success and work
Of fellow-craftsmen in the art divine.

I never felt the sting of hate and envy,
No, no, not even when Puccini charmed
The ears of Paris, nor when first I heard
The moving harmonies of *Iphigenia.*
And who has dared to say that proud Salieri
Ever stooped to envy, played the loathsome snake
That, trampled underfoot, will scatter dust
And sand in helpless rage? No living soul! . . .
But now—this day—I must admit I envy;
This day I own myself an envious man;
I envy deeply, to agony. . . . O heavens!
Where, where is justice when the sacred gift,
When immortality rewards not him
Who serves high art by faithful work and prayer,
With burning love, devotion, self-denial,
But shines with light around a madcap's head,
Upon an idler's brow? . . . O Mozart! Mozart!

(*Mozart enters.*)

MOZART

Oho! You saw me coming! I had in mind
To take you by surprise with something funny.

SALIERI

You here?—When did you come?

MOZART

                              This very minute.
I started out to see you, with some music,
When, passing by a tavern, all at once
I heard a fiddler. . . . I say, my good Salieri,
Upon my word, you never yet have heard

In all your life a thing more comical!
There, in a tavern, a blind old man was playing
My *Voi che sapete*. I simply had to bring
Him here at once, to have him play for you.
Come in!

> (*A blind old man enters with his fiddle.*)

> Play something, play some Mozart, please!

> (*The old man plays aria from* DON GIOVANNI.
> MOZART *roars with laughter.*)

SALIERI

And you can laugh at this?

MOZART

My dear Salieri,
How can you keep from laughing too?

SALIERI

No, no!
I'm not amused to see a clumsy lout
With paint bespatter Raphael's Madonna!
I'm not amused to hear a worthless clown
With parodies dishonor Alighieri! . . .
Be off with you!

MOZART

Wait, here's a little gift
For your pains. Drink to my health.

> (*The old fiddler leaves.*)

Ah, Salieri,
I fear you're out of sorts today. I'll come
Another time.

SALIERI

What music do you bring?

MOZART

Nothing! A trifle only. . . . Somehow last night
I could not fall asleep. Some idle thoughts
Haunted my mind. I set them down this morning
And brought the score. I wanted your opinion.
You are in no mood for me.

SALIERI

Mozart, Mozart!
Your music is my life, my very breath.
Sit down! Play!

MOZART

(*At the piano*)

Well, imagine to yourself
A youth—or me but younger—one in love,
Not deeply, just a little if you please—
Beside a lovely girl or bosom friend . . .
Let's say yourself. . . . I'm happy. All at once—
Visions of gloom and death, that sort of thing.
Now listen.

(*He plays.*)

SALIERI

You were bringing this—to play,
And yet you loitered at a common tavern
To hear a blind old fiddler? Oh, Mozart,
You really don't deserve the soul you have.

MOZART

You like it, do you?

32

SALIERI

How profound your work!
What daring, and what harmony divine!
Mozart, you are a god, and do not know it.
I know, I know it.

MOZART

Well, you may be right.
However, the god in me is getting hungry.

SALIERI

Listen, Mozart, come dine with me tonight
At the Golden Lion.

MOZART

That's very kind, but first
I'd better go and tell my wife I shan't
Be home for dinner.

SALIERI

I'll wait; don't fail me now.

(*Mozart leaves.*)

Ah, no! I can no more resist my fate,
The voice commanding me to stay his flight,
Lest we, high priests and ministers of music,
Not I alone obscure in fame—are lost,
And art as well. What good if Mozart lives
And higher soars on wings outsoaring time?
Will he exalt the plane of art? No, no!
No art endures, unbodied; art will die
Away when he departs and leaves no equal
To take his place. What profit then his life?

A seraph of the skies, he came with songs
Of Paradise—to rouse in mortal clay
But wingless dreams, alas, then fly away.
We'll speed his going; let his spirit soar!

This fatal drug, the gift of dear Isora,
I've cherished eighteen years. How often since
That day life seemed unbearable to me;
How often have I sat at feasts beside
My carefree, unsuspecting enemy,
Yet never did I yield to this temptation,
Although I have no fear of death and brood
Too deeply when I'm wronged. I've waited long.
I've clung to life, despite despair, despite
My thirst for death. I've argued with myself:
Life brings at times some unexpected gift;
Perhaps I shall behold the face of night,
Inspired, and know the rapture of creation;
Perhaps another Haydn will create
New masterworks—new music for my joy. . . .
And when I've feasted with some hated guest,
I've pondered that I soon might meet a foe
Most hateful, that some outrage most accursed
Might rush upon me from some lofty height,—
Then, then I'd need Isora's parting gift.
And I was right! I have discerned at last
That enemy. He came,—another Haydn,
Who found me, filled with ecstasy my life!
Now is the hour! O sacred gift of love,
Lie deep in friendship's cup of wine tonight.

SCENE II

PRIVATE ROOM IN A TAVERN, WITH PIANO

MOZART *and* SALIERI *at table*

SALIERI

What makes you look so gloomy?

MOZART

Gloomy? No.

SALIERI

Yes, Mozart, there is something troubling you.
The dinner's good, the wine is excellent,
But you are glum and mute.

MOZART

I will confess

My *Requiem* is on my mind.

SALIERI

Aha!
You're working on a requiem? Since when?

MOZART

For three weeks past. The case is really strange.
Didn't I tell you?

SALIERI

Why, no.

MOZART

Then listen now.
One night, about three weeks ago, I came
Home late. They told me someone had been there
To see me. I lay all night, I know not why,

Wondering who the caller was, and what
His errand. Then he came a second time.
The following day, when I was playing games
Down on the carpet with my little son,
I heard a voice outside. A tall old man
In black, with courtly bows, commissioned me
To write a requiem, and disappeared.
I set to work at once, but since that day
My visitor in black has never called.
I'm really pleased; I'm loath to part with it,
Although the *Requiem* is done. However . . .

SALIERI

What now?

MOZART

     I am ashamed to say.

SALIERI

         But why?

MOZART

That shape in black disturbs my rest by day
And night. I see his presence everywhere
Around me like a shadow. Even now
I seem to feel him at our table, right
Between us here.

SALIERI

     What childish fears you have!
What foolish fancies! Listen, Beaumarchais
Was wont to say to me: 'My dear Salieri!
When gloomy thoughts assail your peace of mind,

Uncork a bottle of champagne, or else
Read *Figaro*.'

MOZART

Ah, yes! He was your friend.
Of course, you wrote *Tarare* for Beaumarchais.
That music is superb, especially
One tune that I like to hum when I'm happy. . . .
Tra-la-la-la-la! . . . Salieri, is it true
That Beaumarchais did poison anyone?

SALIERI

Nonsense! His sense of humor was too keen
For such a deed as that.

MOZART

You're right. What's more,
He was a genius just like you and me.
Genius and crime are incompatible,
Two worlds apart.

SALIERI

Indeed?

(He drops poison in Mozart's glass.)

Well, Mozart, drink!

MOZART

I drink your health! I drink to honest friendship
That joins the hearts of Mozart and Salieri,
Two sons of harmony.

(He drinks.)

SALIERI

Wait, Mozart, wait!
Wait! You have drunk alone; you left me out.

MOZART

     (Throws down his napkin on the table.)

I've had enough! . . . Salieri, I'll play for you
My *Requiem*.

     (He plays.)

    You're weeping?

SALIERI

                The tears I weep
Are sweet and bitter, tears I've never wept.
Mozart, I feel my dreadful duty's done.
I feel a healing knife has cut from me
Some lacerated member. Mind them not,
My tears, but play again, I beg you, play!
Fill all my soul with sound and airs divine.

MOZART

If men could only feel the spell of music
As you! But, no, the world would fall apart,
For none would care about the common things
We need, in free surrender unto art.
But few are chosen. Few are the happy idlers,
Indifferent to private gain, like priests
Who worship beauty only.—True, my friend?
But I'm not well today! I'm feeling faint.
I must get home, and sleep. So fare you well.

SALIERI

And you fare well!

     (Alone.)

           Forever, Mozart! Sleep. . . .
But is he really right? It cannot be!
I am no genius? . . . And genius and crime

Are worlds apart? . . . But Michelangelo?
It can't be true, it can't! Was then his crime
A foolish legend, an idle tale believed
By vulgar folk alone? And he who built
The Vatican was not—a murderer? . . .

THE
STONE
GUEST

Leporello *O statua gentilissima*
Del gran' Commendatore!
. . . Ah, Padrone!
—Don Giovanni

SCENE I

Don Juan

  We'll wait till nightfall here. We are at last
Before the gateways of Madrid, and soon
Through street familiar long I'll take my way,
My hat pulled safely down, my face concealed.
You think I'll pass? Can I be recognized?

Leporello

  I'm sure no one will find Don Juan out;
The streets are swarming with his kind.

Don Juan

                       You're jesting?

  Well, who would know me?

43

LEPORELLO

                                 Why, any watchman
We chance to meet, some gypsy, drunken fiddler,
Or your own sort—a strutting cavalier
With flowing cloak and sword beneath his arm.

DON JUAN

What matter then? So long as on my way
I do not meet the King himself. In faith,
I fear no other man in all Madrid.

LEPORELLO

And by tomorrow noon the King will hear
Don Juan is back and in Madrid again,
Returned from exile at his own sweet will.
Then what will happen, pray?

DON JUAN

                                He'll turn me back.
He won't cut off my head for this, you know!
My crime was not against the sovereign State!
For my own benefit, to save my life,
He banished me, because the dead man's kin
Had threatened me with death.

LEPORELLO

                                 Just so, just so!
And safe, you should have stayed away for good.

DON JUAN

My humble thanks to you! I all but died
Of boredom there: What people, what a country!
The sky, a pall of smoke! And, oh, their women!
I'd never give, my foolish Leporello,

44

Mark my words, the lowest peasant girl
In Andalusia for all their best
And proudest beauties,—no, I swear I'd not!
I liked them well enough at first for their
Blue eyes, fair skin, and modesty; in fact,
I think it was their charm as something new.
But very soon, thank God, I understood
It was a sin to lose my heart to them,
So prim they are and lifeless! They're no more
Than waxen dolls, not like our girls at home!
But look, I think I recognize this place.

LEPORELLO

No doubt! The convent of Saint Anthony.
We used to come on visits here at night.
I used to guard the horses in this grove
For many unrewarding hours, while you
Were having such a gay good time.

DON JUAN
                        (*Pensively*)
                                    Poor Inez!

She is no more! How greatly I adored her!

LEPORELLO

Inez, with large black eyes! Do I remember!
Three months you sighed and courted her in vain.
'Twas only by the devil's help you won.

DON JUAN

July . . . at midnight. Yes, I used to find
A strange enjoyment in her mournful eyes
And in her ashen lips. So strange it seems,
You did not think her beautiful; perhaps

She had not much of beauty in her face
Except her eyes alone, the light that shone
Within her eyes. I never knew a glance
More wonderful. Her voice was soft and thin,
The voice of pining children. A brutal man
Her husband was, a rogue, I learned too late.
Poor Inez!

LEPORELLO

   But others took her place.

DON JUAN

          I know.

LEPORELLO

And while we live there will be others still.

DON JUAN

 Yes, even so.

LEPORELLO

   What lady in Madrid
Shall we be looking up tonight?

DON JUAN

        Why, Laura!
I'm off to her this very moment!

LEPORELLO

      Right!

DON JUAN

 I'll walk straight in, and if I find another,
I'll speed him through the window on his way.

LEPORELLO

    For certain! Well, I'm glad your gloomy mood
    Has passed, with dead forgotten memories.

(A monk enters.)

    But, look, who's here!

MONK

                    She's coming shortly now.
    And who are you? the guards of Doña Anna?

LEPORELLO

    No, we are gentlemen and strangers, come
    To see Madrid.

DON JUAN

            And whom are you expecting?

MONK

    Good Doña Anna, come to pray upon
    Her husband's grave.

DON JUAN

            De Solva? Doña Anna?
    The wife of the commander slain in a duel?
    Let's see, who was the slayer?

MONK

                   That dissolute,
    That godless libertine Don Juan!

LEPORELLO

              Oho!
    I say, Don Juan's fame has found its way

Even inside the peaceful convent walls,
And holy hermits chant the hero's fame.

MONK

Perhaps you know him?

LEPORELLO

We? Oh, not at all.
But where's the slayer now?

MONK

No longer here;
He's exiled far away.

LEPORELLO

The Lord be praised!
The farther off the better. Still I'd like
All rakes clapped in a sack and pitched into
The sea.

DON JUAN

You're lying!

LEPORELLO

Hush, I'm having fun!

DON JUAN

Then was it here they buried the commander?

MONK

The widow had this monument erected.
She comes each day to weep and pray that God
May grant his soul salvation.

DON JUAN

                         A strange poor widow!
And is the lady pretty?

MONK

                         I am a monk.
And by our vows, fair beauty is a snare.
But lying is a sin; a saint himself
Could not deny her grace and loveliness.

DON JUAN

The dead had, then, good cause for jealousy.
He kept his Doña Anna under lock,
Refusing her companionship and friends.
I'd like the chance to speak to her myself.

MONK

Oh, Doña Anna never speaks these days
With any man.

DON JUAN

             Not even then with you?

MONK

There is a difference: I am a monk.
Now here she comes.

            (Doña Anna enters.)

DOÑA ANNA

            Open the gate, my Father.

MONK

I shall, Señora. I've been expecting you.

          (Doña Anna follows the monk.)

LEPORELLO

Well, what's she like?

DON JUAN

                    I could not see her face
Beneath her widow's veil. But I did note
Her graceful little foot.

LEPORELLO

                    That's quite enough
For you. Your fancy will supply the rest.
Your fancy's nimbler than a painter's brush.
With you it matters little where you start—
The foot or forehead.

DON JUAN

               Listen, Leporello,
I'd like to know the lady.

LEPORELLO

              (*To himself.*)
              Why, he's mad!
The shameless wretch! He killed the husband first
And now seeks pleasure in the widow's tears.

DON JUAN

But see, it's growing dark. Before the moon
Has climbed the city walls and turned the dark
To glowing twilight, let us go at once
Into Madrid.

          (*Don Juan leaves.*)

LEPORELLO

          How like a common thief
The Spanish nobleman. He wants the night

But fears the moon itself. O cursèd life!
How long must I be plagued with him, and keep
How long his pace? My patience's at an end.

SCENE II

FIRST GUEST
    I swear, dear Laura, you have never acted
    With so much true perfection as tonight.
    How thoroughly you understood your role.

SECOND GUEST
    How well conceived, and played with so much power.

THIRD GUEST
    With grace and art.

LAURA
                    Tonight I truly felt
    The meaning of each spoken word, each movement,
    And freely gave myself to inspiration;
    The words came flowing easily as though
    Born of the heart, not slavish memory.

FIRST GUEST
    How true! And now your eyes are shining bright;
    Your glowing cheeks bear witness to the joy
    And ecstasy you feel within yourself.
    Let not your rapture fade away! Give us
    A song, dear Laura!

LAURA

           Hand me my guitar!

           (*Sings.*)

ALL

  Oh, bravo, bravo! Perfect! Marvelous!

FIRST GUEST

  Our thanks to you, enchantress! You have charmed
  Our hearts. Of all delights and joys in life
  To love alone does music yield in sweetness.
  Yet love is melody itself. Don Carlos,
  Our surly evening guest, is also moved.

SECOND GUEST

What wealth of sound! What passion it reveals.
Who wrote the words, dear Laura?

LAURA

Don Juan.

DON CARLOS

Don Juan? He?

LAURA

Some time or other, he,
My faithful friend but my inconstant lover.

DON CARLOS

Your Don Juan is a godless reprobate
And you're a little fool.

LAURA

Have you gone mad?
I'll call my men and bid them cut your throat,
Grandee or no grandee.

DON CARLOS

(*Rises up.*)

Well, let them come!

FIRST GUEST

No, Laura, no! Don Carlos, don't be angry!

LAURA

Don Juan honorably killed his brother,
In single combat. Better far he'd killed
Don Carlos!

DON CARLOS

      'Twas my fault, my foolish anger.

LAURA

Now since you own your words to me were foolish,
Let us be friends again.

DON CARLOS

               Forgive me, Laura,
I do admit my fault. You know yourself
I cannot bear the mention of that name.

LAURA

Am I to blame because his name is now
As ever dear to me?

A GUEST

             To prove you are
No longer angry and in sign of peace,
Come, Laura, sing another song.

LAURA

               I'll sing
A farewell song. The hour is late. What shall
I sing? Ah, listen!

(Sings)

ALL

      Charming! How sublime!

LAURA

Good night, my friends!

GUESTS

      Good night, and thank you, Laura!

(Guests depart. Laura stops Don Carlos.)

LAURA

You savage, you! Remain with me tonight.
You took my fancy, flaring up like that;
You brought Don Juan to my mind again
The way you railed at me and set your teeth.

DON CARLOS

The lucky man! You loved him?

(*Laura nods.*)

Deeply?

LAURA

Yes.

DON CARLOS

You love him deeply still?

LAURA

This very minute?
Ah, no! I cannot love two men at once.
'Tis you I love at present.

DON CARLOS

Tell me, Laura,
How old are you?

LAURA

I'm eighteen now, my friend.

DON CARLOS

O Laura, you're so young, and will be young
For five or six years longer. Six years more
At best our men will worship you in crowds,

And shower you with presents and caresses,
With flattery and serenades of love
At night. They'll fight for your dear sake in duels
On city squares. But soon the time will come
When wrinkles of old age will mar your brow.
Your eyes will lose their brightness; silver threads
Will streak the darkness of your raven hair,
And men will cast you off as one grown old.
What then? What do you say?

LAURA

Why fret about
The future now? What novel conversation!
Or do you always brood so gloomily?—
Come to the balcony. Here let us sit.
How calm the sky! The air is warm and still;
The night is sweet with lemon and with laurel;
The moon is shining in the dark-blue deep,
And only watchmen cry their lone 'All's well.'
But maybe in the north, in Paris, now
The sky is overcast with clouds, the winds
Are blowing hard, and rains are falling cold.
But we must have no care.—Don Carlos, smile
At me. I order you to smile at me! . . .
That's better.

DON CARLOS

Lovely demon!

(*Knocking at the door.*)

DON JUAN

Laura, ho!

LAURA

What't that? Whose voice is that I hear?

DON JUAN

Open!

LAURA

Great heavens! . . . He?

(*Opens the door.*)

DON JUAN

Good evening!

LAURA

Don Juan!

(*She throws her arms about his neck.*)

DON CARLOS

What! Don Juan?

DON JUAN

My Laura, dearest love!

(*Kisses her.*)

Whom have you here, my Laura?

DON CARLOS

I, Don Carlos.

DON JUAN

An unexpected meeting! Well, I'll be
Tomorrow at your service.

DON CARLOS

No, this minute!

LAURA

    Don Carlos, stop, I say! You're in my house,
    Not in a public square! I beg you, leave!

DON CARLOS

                    (Not listening to her.)

    I'm waiting. Well? You have your sword with you.

DON JUAN

    If you insist, I will. . . .

                   (They fight.)

LAURA

                  Oh, oh! Don Juan!

   (Throws herself on the couch. Don Carlos falls.)

DON JUAN

Rise, Laura, rise! It's done.

LAURA

                    Don Carlos dead?
How lovely—in my room! What shall I do,
You scapegrace devil? Where can I put him?

DON JUAN

Perhaps he's still alive.

                    (*Examining the body.*)

LAURA

                    Alive? You wretch,
Just look at him! You pierced him through the heart.
His blood no longer flows; his breath has stopped.
How could you?

DON JUAN

                    Laura, I am not to blame.
He dared me to the duel.

LAURA

                    Oh, Don Juan!
You're always up to pranks, and always not
At fault. But tell me where you come from now?
How long have you been here?

DON JUAN

                              I've just returned,
In secrecy. I had no right to come.

LAURA

And you remembered Laura first of all?
For that, I'm glad. I don't believe you, no!
You happened to be passing near by chance
And saw my house.

DON JUAN

No, Laura! I am lodged
Outside the city in a wretched inn.
Ask Leporello. For your sake alone
I came into Madrid.

(*Kisses her.*)

LAURA

My dearest boy!
Stop . . . not before the dead! What shall we do?

DON JUAN

Let him lie there. Before the break of day
I'll take him with me, hidden in my cloak,
And drop him at a cross-road.

LAURA

Only take
Good care that no one sees you. 'Tis your luck
You did not come a minute earlier!
I had your friends at supper here with me
A while ago. Suppose you'd met them here!

DON JUAN

How long, my Laura, have you loved that man?

LAURA

Loved him? You must be raving!

DON JUAN

                              Come, confess
  How many times you've been unfaithful since
  I left?

LAURA

                Scapegrace, and what about yourself?

DON JUAN
  Confess it, Laura! . . . No, some other time!

SCENE III

THE COMMANDER'S MONUMENT

DON JUAN
  It's worked out well! Since having slain by chance
  Don Carlos, I've taken refuge here, concealed
  In humble hermit's guise, and here each day
  I see my charming widow. I dare to think
  I've won her true regard; till now we have
  Remained on formal terms. But I will speak
  To her spontaneously and plain at last.
  Shall I then say, "May I presume?" or greet
  Her with "Señora?" Bah! I'll say what comes
  Into my head. I'll speak with frankness, simply,
  Like one whose serenade is improvised.
  'Tis time she came. Her absence makes the stone
  Commander seem so lone. They've made him look
  Big-shouldered, giant-like, a Hercules!
  And yet he was, poor chap, so small and puny

That, standing here on tiptoe with his arms
Held high, he'd scarcely reach the statue's nose.
The time we met at Escurial together,
I pricked him with my sword, and there he lay,
A dragonfly transfixed upon a pin.
Still he was proud and bold, a rugged man
In spirit. . . . Ah, she comes!

DoÑa Anna

(*Aside; then to the monk.*)

He's here again.
Forgive me, Father, if I have disturbed
Your meditation.

Don Juan

No, 'tis I who must,
Señora, pray forgiveness, for perhaps
My presence hinders you in your great grief.

DoÑa Anna

No, Father, for my grief lies buried deep.
My humble prayer will in your presence here
Ascend to Heaven peacefully. I beg
You join your voice and prayer with my appeal.

Don Juan

To pray together—you and I alone?
I am unworthy of so great an honor.
I cannot venture with unholy lips
Your holy supplication to repeat;
I can but look from far with reverence
On you, when, as you kneel in prayer, your head
Lies mournfully upon the pallid marble,

And then it seems to me an angel blest
Has visited this tomb. Nor dare I hope
To find a prayer in this, my troubled heart.
I stand in silent wonder and I think
How blessed is the man whose cold marble
Glows with a widow's warm celestial breath
And tears of her eternal love in death.

DOÑA ANNA
    Strange words are these!

DON JUAN
                    Señora?

DOÑA ANNA
                            You have forgotten—

DON JUAN
    That I'm a lowly monk and that my voice
    Must not resound thus freely in this place?

DOÑA ANNA
    It seems to me . . . I do not understand . . .

DON JUAN
    Ah, I see you have guessed my secret heart!

DOÑA ANNA
    What secret, please?

DON JUAN
                    No hermit monk the man
    Who lowly craves forgiveness at your feet!

DOÑA ANNA
    O Heavens! Rise at once! Who are you then?

DON JUAN

A hapless victim of my hopeless love.

DOÑA ANNA

O God in Heaven! Before this tomb? Leave me!

DON JUAN

One minute, Doña Anna!

DOÑA ANNA

We could be seen! . . .

DON JUAN

The gate is locked. Grant me a single word.

DOÑA ANNA

What is it that you wish this minute?

DON JUAN

Death!
Oh, let me die this minute at your feet,
And let my wretched dust lie buried here—
O not beside the dust of him you love—
Not near him—but a little distance off,
Beside the gates perchance, at the threshold.
And there the stone upon my grave may feel
Your footfall or the rustling of your dress
When hither you will come to pray before
This lofty monument and, silent, weep.

DOÑA ANNA

You've surely lost your mind.

DON JUAN

Doña Anna!

What madness this—my yearning for the end?
Were I but mad, I'd have a strong desire
To stay alive with you and keep the hope
Someday to move your heart with tender love;
Were I but mad, I'd watch your balcony,
I'd keep long vigils, haunt your sleep with song.
I would not hide from you were I but mad.
I'd seek to live each moment in your sight,
And never in the world consent to suffer
So in silence.

DOÑA ANNA

             You've proved your silence well.

DON JUAN

A happy chance has tempted me to speak,
Doña Anna, or ne'er would you have known
Of this, the mournful secret of my heart.

DOÑA ANNA

And have you been in love with me for long?

DON JUAN

How long in love with you I do not know.
But since the time I came to feel how good
My earthly days might be, I realized
The truth and shape of happiness in life.

DOÑA ANNA

Leave me: I fear to stay alone with you.

DON JUAN

You fear, with me?

Doña Anna

                    Your words arouse my fears.

Don Juan

I'll ask no more, but do not banish me
Who, in your presence, finds his only joy.
I do not dare foolhardily to hope;
I ask no favor, if you doom me thus,
Except to see you.

Doña Anna

                  Leave me! Not this the place
For words like yours, for madness such as yours.
Come tomorrow, and if you'll vow at first

To guard my person with all reverence,
I shall receive you—in the evening, late,—
Though I have kept myself apart in life
Since I was widowed.

DON JUAN

                Angel! Doña Anna!
God bless and comfort you as you today
Have comforted one hapless sufferer.

DOÑA ANNA

And now you must depart.

DON JUAN

                   One moment, one.

DOÑA ANNA

No more. I cannot stay. Besides, I'm not
Inclined to praying now. Your words of love,
To which my ears have long, long been unused,
Have turned me from my task. Tomorrow then
I will receive you.

DON JUAN

                I can scarcely dare
Believe my happiness is true! Tomorrow,
At evening then, not here, and not by stealth!

DOÑA ANNA

Tomorrow, yes, tomorrow. And your name?

DON JUAN

Diego de Calvado.

DOÑA ANNA

          Don Diego,
  Farewell.

               (*Exit.*)

DON JUAN

        Leporello!

        (*Leporello enters.*)

LEPORELLO

             What now your pleasure?

DON JUAN

  My dearest Leporello! Oh, I'm happy!
  Tomorrow, late, when evening comes! Tomorrow,
  Tomorrow, Leporello! Be prepared!
  I'm happy as a child.

LEPORELLO

              You spoke with her?
  Perhaps she said a few kind words, no more,
  Or maybe you have given her your blessing.

DON JUAN

  No, Leporello, no! 'Tis an appointment,
  A real appointment at her house for me!

LEPORELLO

  Really? Oh, widows! you are all alike.

DON JUAN

  I'm wild with joy! I want to sing for joy!

LEPORELLO

  But what will the Commander say to this?

DON JUAN

    You think he will be jealous? He's a man
    Of common sense, grown wise since he is dead.

LEPORELLO

    No, look upon that statue there!

DON JUAN

                          Well, what?

LEPORELLO

    I fear he looks with anger there at you.

DON JUAN

    Well speak, good Leporello, speak to it,
    And bid it come tomorrow to my house—
    To Doña Anna's house, tomorrow night.

LEPORELLO

    Invite the statue? Why?

DON JUAN

                    Well, rest assured
    I don't intend to keep it company.
    Ask the statue to come to Doña Anna's
    Tomorrow late at night, to stand on guard
    Alone before her door.

LEPORELLO

                You're jesting; think!

DON JUAN

    I bid you go!

LEPORELLO

        But . . .

DON JUAN

                  Go, I tell you now!

LEPORELLO

Most wonderful, O statue great in fame!
My master, Don Juan, invites you humbly
To come . . . Good Lord, I cannot, I am afraid!

DON JUAN

Coward! I'll make you do it.

LEPORELLO

                      Very well.
My master, Don Juan, invites you humbly
To stand on guard outside your widow's door
Tomorrow night.

(The Statue nods.)

          Ah, Ah!

DON JUAN

                What now?

LEPORELLO

                   Ah, ah!
Oh, God! I'll die!

DON JUAN

           What ails you, fool!

LEPORELLO

          (Nodding.)
                  The statue!

DON JUAN

Are you inviting it?

LEPORELLO

The statue, look!

DON JUAN

What folly! Why, you're mad!

LEPORELLO

Then try yourself.

DON JUAN

Well, look, you knave!

(*To the statue.*)

My Lord, I bid you come
Tomorrow to your widow's house, to stand
On guard before the door. Then will you come?

(*Statue nods.*)

Oh, heavens!

LEPORELLO

Well, I told you! . . .

DON JUAN

Come! Let's go!

SCENE IV

DOÑA ANNA'S ROOM

DON JUAN *and* DOÑA ANNA

DOÑA ANNA

I gave, Don Diego, my consent to have
You come tonight, and yet I fear my talk
And grief might weary you. Alone I bear

My loss, but like a day in spring, I cry
And smile. Why so silent?

DON JUAN

                        Too glad for words,
I deeply muse on being here alone
With you, O lovely Doña Anna,—not there
Beside the tombstone of the happy dead.
I joy not seeing you upon your knees
Before a stony spouse.

DOÑA ANNA

                    Oh, Don Diego,
Are you so jealous that the graves torment
Your mind?

DON JUAN

          There is no room for jealousy.
Your husband was your own free choice.

DOÑA ANNA

                         Ah, no!
My mother bade me marry Don Alvaro,
For we were poor, and Don Alvaro, rich.

DON JUAN

O happy man! He spread his wealth before
The shrine of beauty, and with empty gold
He won the bliss of paradise. Had I
But known you first, I'd have bestowed on you
My rank, estate, my wealth, and life itself
With rapture, all for one sweet smile from you.
Your slave, each little whim of yours I would
Have tried to understand and gratify

Before you'd told your wish, that all your life
Might be one everlasting fairy dream.
But Heaven granted me a sadder fate.

Doña Anna

Ah, Diego, say no more! 'Tis wrong of me
To listen since I dare not give my love;
I must be faithful even to the dead.
If you but knew how Don Alvaro loved me!
Had he been left a widower, I'm sure
He'd never have received a lovelorn lady
In his great loyalty to me.

Don Juan

                    I pray you,
O Doña Anna, torture me no more,
Remembering the dead. Have pity then,
Although I well deserve your punishment.

Doña Anna

But why? You're free, not bound by holy ties
To anyone. In loving me, you do
No wrong at all in Heaven's eyes or mine!

Don Juan

In yours! . . . O God!

Doña Anna

                  But are you guilty then
Of any wrong to me? Do tell me, why?

Don Juan

Never!

DOÑA ANNA

            Diego, tell me what you mean!
How have you wronged me, that you blame yourself?

DON JUAN

   No, not for worlds!

DOÑA ANNA

                  Diego, this is strange.
I ask you, I demand it now.

DON JUAN

             No, no!

DOÑA ANNA

   Is this your blind obedience to my will?
And did you not so hotly proffer me
Just now to be my very slave for life?
I feel the hurt you give, Diego. Answer:
For what great wrong to me are you to blame?

DON JUAN

   I dare not say a word, or you would hate
Me then.

DOÑA ANNA

           But I forgive you from the first,
And yet I wish to know.

DON JUAN

               Ah, do not ask
To hear my horrible, my fateful secret.

DOÑA ANNA

   Fateful! Your words are wild and fill my heart
With pain. I wait in fear and want to know

The nature of your harm and wrong to me.
We'd never met; I have no enemies,
And never had, except the man who killed
My husband.

DON JUAN

(*Aside.*)

Now the secret must be told.
Please tell me, frankly, did you ever meet
Poor Don Juan?

DOÑA ANNA

No, never in my life.

DON JUAN

But in your inmost heart you hate that man?

DOÑA ANNA

I'm honor bound. But you are trying hard
To turn aside my question, Don Diego.
But I demand, I must . . .

DON JUAN

Suppose that you
Should chance somehow to meet Don Juan?

DOÑA ANNA

I'd plunge
My dagger in his heart!

DON JUAN

Doña Anna,
Where now your dagger? Here's my naked breast!

DOÑA ANNA

Diego!

DON JUAN

No, not Diego. I'm Don Juan.

DOÑA ANNA

O God . . . You play with me; I don't believe.

DON JUAN

I'm Don Juan.

DOÑA ANNA

No, no!

DON JUAN

'Tis I who killed
Your husband, nor do I regret my deed,
Nor feel the sting of penitence or wrong.

DOÑA ANNA

What do I hear? No, no, it can't be true!

DON JUAN

I'm Don Juan. I love you.

DOÑA ANNA

(*Fainting.*)

Where am I? . . .
Where? Oh, I'm ill, so faint!

DON JUAN

What have I done?
What is the matter, Doña Anna? Come,
Wake up, arouse yourself! I am your slave,
Your Diego's at your feet.

DOÑA ANNA

(*Weakly.*)

Leave me alone.

You are my enemy; you took away
All, all I had in life. . . .

DON JUAN

Oh, my dearest!

If only for my crimes I could atone,
I'd wait upon your sentence at your feet.
I'll die if that's your wish; or bid me live
For you alone. . . .

DOÑA ANNA

Then you are Don Juan.

DON JUAN

I'm sure he's often been described to you
As scoundrel, monster, rogue. O Doña Anna,
There is perhaps some truth in hearsay tales.
Perhaps a heavy weight of evil lies
Upon my conscience. True, for long I've been
The willing slave of lust. But since I first
Saw you, it seems I have been born again,
And loving you, I am in love with virtue.
And now in humility I kneel at last
Before all excellence on trembling knees.

DOÑA ANNA

Ah, yes, I've heard Don Juan's eloquent.
I've heard he is a man of evil, guile,
That he's a godless man, an arrant fiend.
How many women have you sent to their
Great misery?

DON JUAN

                    Believe, not one among
Those women have I loved.

DOÑA ANNA

                              Must I believe
Don Juan is in love at last, that I
Am not just one more victim of his lust?

DON JUAN

Had I desired but only to deceive you,
Would I confess, reveal my name to you,
A name that you can scarcely bear to hear?
I pray you, where my guile, my craftiness?

DOÑA ANNA

Who knows your heart? . . . How is it that you dared
To come into this house? Here any man
Might know your face at once and kill at sight.

DON JUAN

But why fear death? For one sweet meeting here
With you, I'll uncomplaining give my life.

DOÑA ANNA

Imprudent man, how can you leave this house?

DON JUAN

(*Kissing her hand.*)
You then do care for me—the life of poor
Don Juan! Then you do not hate me now
In your angelic soul, O Doña Anna?

DOÑA ANNA

Alas! I wish I had the strength to hate!
But we must part.

DON JUAN

When shall we meet again?

DOÑA ANNA

Another time; I do not know.

DON JUAN

Tomorrow?

DOÑA ANNA

Where?

DON JUAN

Here.

DOÑA ANNA

How weak my woman's heart, Don Juan!

DON JUAN

One parting kiss, your token of forgiveness.

DOÑA ANNA

No, no! 'Tis late.

DON JUAN

Just one, one kiss of peace.

DOÑA ANNA

How teasingly you ask. Then kiss me—once.
(Knocking.)
What noise is that? Oh hide, Don Juan, quick!

DON JUAN

Farewell, my dearest, till we meet again!
(Goes out, and runs in again.)
Oh! . . .

DOÑA ANNA

What's the matter? Oh! . . .
(The statue enters. Doña Anna faints.)

STATUE

You bade me come.

DON JUAN

O God! O Doña Anna!

STATUE

Leave her now.
This is the end. Don Juan is not afraid?

DON JUAN

No, no! I bade you come. I'm glad you've come.

STATUE

Give me your hand.

DON JUAN

My hand I give to you. . . .
Oh, hard his hand, his mighty hand of stone!
Oh, let me go! Enough! Let go my hand! . . .
I'm dying—all is over! O Doña Anna!
(*They sink into the ground.*)

A FEAST
DURING
THE PLAGUE

A Street. A Table Laid for a Feast. A Group
of Men and Women

YOUNG MAN

Your honor, Mr. Chairman! Let me here
Remind you of a man we all knew well,
A man whose quips and entertaining stories,
Whose pointed repartee and observations
So caustic in their mock solemnity,
Cheered happily our table talk. He helped
To chase away our deepest gloom that now
Our visitor, the Plague, begins to cast
Upon the brightest minds and wits among us.
But two days past, we hailed his puns and tales
With merry laughter. Sir, it will be wrong
If we forget, rejoicing in our feast
Today, our good old Jackson. Here's his chair,
The empty chair that seems to be awaiting
Our friend and wag—our friend who left us for
That chilly dwelling-place beneath the earth.

There never was so eloquent a tongue
And brave, remembered even in his doom;
We here, the living many, have no cause
To yield to hopeless grief. Let me propose
We drink a toast to Jackson's memory
With joyful clanging glasses, gay applause,
As though he were alive.

CHAIRMAN

                                    He was the first
To leave our ranks. In silence let us drink
In honor of his name.

YOUNG MAN

                              Have it your way.

(They lift their glasses in silence.)

CHAIRMAN

Your voice, my dear, interprets well the accents
Of native songs in all their wild perfection:
Sing, Mary, something very sad and plaintive
That we may then partake of this, our feast,
With greater mirth, like men but briefly turned
Aside from life and light by some dark vision.

MARY

(Sings.)

In days long past our land
Was lovely to behold;
To church on holy days
Came all the young and old.
Our children were at school

Or noisily at play,
And reapers harvested
The golden grain and hay.

But now the church is dark;
No children on the green;
In empty field and mead
There's not a reaper seen.
Deserted stands each cottage
And wasted every glade,
But in the graveyard lone
The sound of pick and spade.

New corpses every hour
They bring with fear and dread,
And mourners, weeping, pray
God's mercy for the dead.
There's never room enough
Where all the dead may sleep,
And graves must huddle close
Like many frightened sheep.

And if it be my fate
To die within the night,
Then, for my sake and love,
O Edmund, my delight,
I pray you do not mourn
Your bride too near, too near,
But follow from afar
Poor Jenny in her bier.

Ah, fare you well, my own,
Afar from this decay,
In sweeter peace and cheer
Forget this mournful day.
Come back in future days,
Come where my body lies;
Poor Jenny then will smile
On Edmund from the skies.

CHAIRMAN

We thank you, Mary, for your pensive air;
We thank you for your tender, mournful song.
In days long past a plague as fierce as ours
Once visited your native hills and valleys,
And there lamentations pitifully rose
Along the banks of many brooks and streams
That still flow gay and shining now in peace
Throughout your paradise of moors and woods.
'Tis true the gloomy year when many died,
So many brave and good and noble souls,
Has left no more than brief vague memories
In simple shepherd songs of pleasing air
And plaintive tune. No, nothing, I believe,
Makes sadder now our day and merriment
Than pensive sounds remembered, known by heart.

MARY

Oh, had I never come to sing at all
Beyond the village hut where I was born!
My parents loved to hear their Mary sing;
Even now it seems I hear myself in song
Still singing in the doorway of our home:

In former days my voice had sweeter sound,
The golden voice of innocence.

LOUISE
                    Your songs
Are out of fashion, dear, yet one may find
A few kind souls who weaken at the sight
Of women's tears, and blindly trust their tears.
Such women think their tearful faces most
Enchanting; if by chance they could believe
That laughter suits them best, they'd smile to please
At any moment. Walsingham has spoken
In praise of shrilling northern beauties,—hence,
They sigh and wail only to please. I hate
That flaxen yellow of those Scottish heads!

CHAIRMAN
Listen! I hear the sound of heavy wheels.

(*Driven by a Negro, a cart piled high with the dead.*)

Aha! She's fainted! From her railing tongue
Alone I thought she had a mannish heart.
Not so! for cruelty is often weaker
Than tender kindliness, and abject fears
Abide in hearts of passion. Water, Mary,
Throw water in her face! She's better now.

MARY
O sister of my sorrow and my shame!
Come, rest your head on me.

LOUISE
                (*Regaining her senses.*)
                    A dreadful demon

In a dream appeared to me—all black except
His whitish eyes. He beckoned me to come
Where, in his cart, the dead lay muttering
Some fearful words I could not understand.
And was it but a dream?—Oh tell me, please,
Has the cart really passed?

YOUNG MAN

        Cheer up, Louise!
Although our street's a quiet hiding-place,
And safe from death, our haunt of revelry
By noise untroubled, yet those rumbling wheels
Have a right of thoroughfare in any street;
It is their privilege. Friend Walsingham,
Let's turn from strife and women's fainting spells!
Give us a song, a reckless, lively song,—
No tale or sighs that tell of Scottish grief,
But something wild, a bacchanalian song
Inspired by friendship and the flaming wine!

CHAIRMAN

Such songs I do not have, but let me sing
A hymn in honor of the Plague. I wrote
This hymn last evening after we had parted.
I felt the need, the first in all my life,
To write in rhyming lines. My husky voice,
As you will hear, suits well this kind of song.

VOICES

A hymn! A hymn! Let's hear the Chairman sing
In honor of the Plague! Bravo! Bravo!

CHAIRMAN

(*Sings.*)

When fearlessly King Winter swoops
Upon us with his hoary troops,
And brings against us in his ire
A mighty host of frost and snow,
Then we will gather at the fire
And feast with cups of wine aglow.

She comes to us, a greedy guest,
Herself, her majesty Queen Pest,
To gorge upon the sick and slain.
By day and night her graveyard spade
She raps upon each window-pane.
Where can we turn, and whence our aid?

The way we meet the Winter's tide
So let us meet the Plague outside—
With light, with lights ablaze, and wine!
And so with laughter and with jest
Come dance and drink, with praise divine
To hail her majesty Queen Pest!

There's bliss in savage war, and bliss
Above the dreadful black abyss;
There's bliss upon the raging main
Among the plunging seas, with death,
In the wild Arabian hurricane,
And in the Plague's corrupted breath.

All, all the fears that would destroy
Give mortal man the greatest joy

And secret bliss that overflow
Our senses with immortal life!
And happy are the men who know
The ecstasy of storm and strife.

And so, O Plague, we hail thy reign!
We laugh at graves, at death and pain.

We die no cowards in the night!
We drink, carefree! The baneful breath
Of dying beauty's our delight,—
Our daring in the face of Death!

(*Old clergyman enters.*)

CLERGYMAN

What godless feast, O godless sons of folly!
By your indecent songs and revelry
You here offend the fearful night of silence
Spread everywhere by death! Among the mourners
In dreadful sorrow deep, among pale faces
About me in the graveyard where I kneel
And pray, each hour your hateful gaiety
And orgies mock the peace of silent graves,
And rock the very earth above the dead.
Had not the prayers of women and old men
Hallowed our common grave of brotherhood,
I might have thought exulting fiends torment
All sinners lost tonight and drag them down
With fiendish laughter to eternal darkness.

VOICES

How masterful his narrative of hell!
Pass on, old fellow! Mind your own affairs.

CLERGYMAN

But I beseech you by the holy blood
Of Him who suffered on the Cross for our
Salvation, stop this monstrous feast if you
Have hope to meet the souls of your beloved
In life eternal. Go, go to your homes!

CHAIRMAN

Our homes are dismal. Youth is fond of mirth.

CLERGYMAN

You, Walsingham? the man who, but three weeks
Ago, was on his knees, embracing close

His mother's corpse? the man who rocked and wailed
With weeping bitterly above her grave?
Do you then think she does not grieve for you,
Grieve bitterly even among the blessed,
As she beholds her son with revellers,
At wanton feasts of wine and lust, and hears
His voice in shameless singing, torn between
His broken sighs and purest prayers to God?
Arise, and follow me!

CHAIRMAN
                  Why do you come
To trouble me? My place is here today.
Here I am held by dreadful memories,
Despair, the knowledge of my lawless ways,
By fear and horror of the deathly void
That meets me when I come into my house.
My place is here: I like their revelry,
Their riot, drinking—God forgive me—and
The wanton love of fallen simple creatures.
My mother's soul can summon me no more.
Too late I hear your voice; too late your help,
Too late your message of salvation calls
Unto my soul. Depart in peace, old man,
And cursed be anyone who follows you.

VOICES
Bravo! Well spoken, noble chairman, bravo!
You've heard his sermon, father! Off with you!

CLERGYMAN
Mathilda's sainted spirit calls to you.

CHAIRMAN

(Rises.)

No, promise me, and raise your withered hand
To heaven! Promise you will leave in peace
Her name forever silenced in the grave!
O that I could conceal this savage feast
From her immortal eyes! There was a time
She thought my spirit pure and free and proud,
And my embrace—her paradise on earth. . . .
Where am I?—O holy child of light! Your soul's
Above me in a realm where for my sins
I cannot rise.

A WOMAN'S VOICE

         These fits again! The fool
Still raves about his wife long dead and buried.

CLERGYMAN

Come, follow me!

CHAIRMAN

         In God's name, holy father,
Let me be.

CLERGYMAN

         May God have mercy on your soul.
Farewell, my son.

    (The clergyman departs. The feast continues. The
    chairman remains seated, sunk in deep thought.)